Today Is Christmas!

by P. K. Hallinan

ideals children's books™

Nashville, Tennessee

ISBN 0-8249-5329-0 (case)
ISBN 0-8249-5330-4 (paper)

Published by Ideals Children's Books
An imprint of Ideals Publications
A division of Guideposts
535 Metroplex Drive, Suite 250
Nashville, Tennessee 37211
www.idealspublications.com

Printed and bound in Mexico by R. R. Donnelley & Sons.

Library of Congress CIP data on file.

For Michael and Nicholas Wilkie

Other Books by P. K. Hallinan

10 8 6 4 2   3 5 7 9

It's Christmas today
and you wake up so fast—
it's hard to believe
that it's Christmas at last!

But it's still very dark,
so you stay curled in bed,
with scenes of the season
aswirl in your head.

It started with shopping
some four weeks ago.
Hot popcorn was popping;
there was holly and snow.

The stores were all glowing
with windows that gleamed
like fantasy kingdoms
in winterland dreams.

And the toys whirred around
making wonderful sounds.

Of course, you remember
how you waited in line
to visit with Santa—
what a dazzling time!

Oh, Santa was jolly!
And he listened well too.
Then an elf with a camera
took a snapshot of you.

So you smiled and chose
a "best friends" kind of pose.

There was mist in the air
the night that you searched
through a Christmas tree lot
for the best tree on earth.

But there your tree stood,
so small and alone
that it practically begged you
to take it back home.

So you shouted with glee
"Can we please have this tree?"

You covered your tree
with tinsel and lights,
with ornaments and candy canes—
oh my, what a sight!

On the mantel you placed
a nativity scene
with Joseph and Mary,
and the Christ Child between.

And a star up above
shone with radiant love.

Oh, what a season!
What a wonderful spell!
There were carolers singing
such joyous noels.

And the holiday feeling
spread through the whole town
with warm-hearted greetings
and jingle-bell sounds.

And the days slowly passed,
bringing Christmas Eve at last.

The candlelight service
was graced with a prayer
while friendship and love
filled the holiday air.

Back home you wrapped presents
made specially for friends,
using ribbon and paper
and taping each end.

And they came out just right,
with the bows good and tight.

But the last thing you did
before going to bed
was hang up your stocking
with a short note that said,

"Santa, we've left out
some cookies for you.
Thank you for all of
the nice things you do."

Then with nary a peep
you went right to sleep.

Now, finally it's daylight!
It's time to go see
what Santa Claus left for you
under the tree!

Oh, what a vision!
What a sight to behold!
The room seems to shimmer
like silver and gold!

Now, what's that you spy
at the foot of the tree?
Why, it's presents for you
and your whole family!

And can it be true?
Your stocking's full too!

Soon the room's brimming
with laughter and smiles.
Hot cider is simmering;
the gifts are in piles.

And the best gift of all
is the joy that you share
as the spirit of Christmas
fills everyone there.

Later that day
your friends gather near
to show you what Santa Claus
brought them this year.

Then you lovingly trade
the gifts that you made.

Too soon you head home,
for time's running late.
You have relatives coming
and dinner won't wait.

So you say a farewell
to your friends, good and true . . .

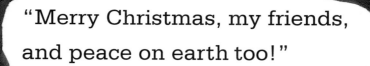

"Merry Christmas, my friends, and peace on earth too!"